AUTHOR'S NOTE

The legend of Spotted Eagle & Black Crow was told over a hundred years ago by Red Cloud, the great Lakota chief in the days before gold prospectors and the U.S. Cavalry invaded the Black Hills.

In 1967, on Rosebud Indian Reservation, Jenny Leading Cloud told the story of Spotted Eagle & Black Crow to storyteller and artist Richard Erdoes. The Lakota tale found its way into the invaluable pages of *American Indian Myths and Legends*, published in 1984 by Pantheon Books and edited by Erdoes and Alfonso Ortiz.

In my version of this story, I've magnified the conflict between Spotted Eagle and Black Crow by making them brothers. Spotted Eagle — named after the Great Spirit's winged messenger — receives his eagle powers in a dream-vision that dramatizes his reverence for the sacred and reminds us of what Lakota children have always been taught: that we are related to all living things.

Special thanks to C.R. Salaz, who helped me cross the bridge to Turtle Island. I am also grateful to Wendell Deer With Horns, my first Lakota reader, and to Virginia Driving Hawk Sneve, for her comments on the text and artwork.

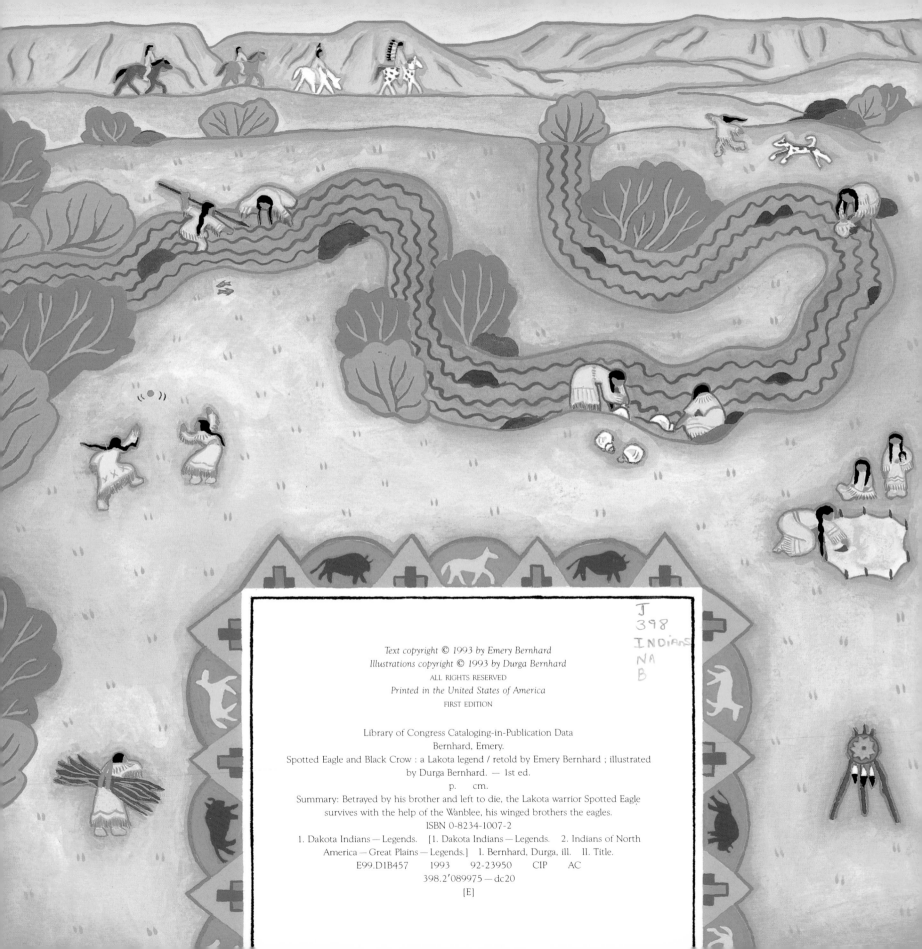

Text copyright © 1993 by Emery Bernhard
Illustrations copyright © 1993 by Durga Bernhard
ALL RIGHTS RESERVED
Printed in the United States of America
FIRST EDITION

Library of Congress Cataloging-in-Publication Data
Bernhard, Emery.
Spotted Eagle and Black Crow : a Lakota legend / retold by Emery Bernhard ; illustrated
by Durga Bernhard. — 1st ed.
p.   cm.
Summary: Betrayed by his brother and left to die, the Lakota warrior Spotted Eagle
survives with the help of the Wanblee, his winged brothers the eagles.
ISBN 0-8234-1007-2
1. Dakota Indians — Legends. [1. Dakota Indians — Legends.   2. Indians of North
America — Great Plains — Legends.]   I. Bernhard, Durga, ill.   II. Title.
E99.D1B457   1993   92-23950   CIP   AC
398.2'089975 — dc20
[E]

SPOTTED EAGLE
&
BLACK CROW

A LAKOTA LEGEND

RETOLD BY
EMERY BERNHARD

ILLUSTRATED BY
DURGA BERNHARD

HOLIDAY HOUSE • NEW YORK

For Jonah,
a warrior
from birth

This happened long ago,
before the white man used his rifle
to kill *Wanblee*, the eagle,
before the white man stamped
eagles on his silver coins,
before the prairie earth was
stitched with railway ties
and churned to dust
by wagon wheels . . .

This is the story of
Spotted Eagle and Black Crow.

SPOTTED EAGLE AND BLACK CROW were brothers. Both were brave warriors, and both loved the same woman. Her name was Red Bird.

On a cool evening in the Moon of the Grass Appearing, Red Bird listened to Spotted Eagle playing his flute. The music was as sweet as the breeze off a summer meadow.

Black Crow heard the music, too. As he listened he thought, "Red Bird will never marry me as long as my brother is alive. I must get rid of him."

The next day, Black Crow said to Spotted Eagle, "It's time to go on a war party against the Pawnee. They stole our best ponies on their last raid."

Spotted Eagle nodded. "Yes, we need good horses for the buffalo hunt. I will go with you."

Spotted Eagle and Black Crow left on a warm day in the Moon When the Ponies Shed. They rode quietly into Pawnee territory, watching for signs of the enemy.

Late in the afternoon, Spotted Eagle saw two Pawnee warriors in the distance. "We must be sure they haven't seen us," said Black Crow. "Let's spy on them."

Black Crow led the way to a high bluff and crawled to the edge. The Pawnee had disappeared. "Look," he said, pointing straight down the cliff. "An eagle's nest with two young ones. Let's kill them. Their feathers will give us power!"

"No!" said Spotted Eagle. "Eagle feathers must be earned. Lower me down with my rope. I will take feathers from the nest."

As soon as Spotted Eagle landed on the ledge, his brother let go of the rope. "Don't worry!" shouted Black Crow. "I'll tell our people you died the death of a warrior! Red Bird won't mourn forever."

Black Crow walked away, ignoring his brother's cries.

Spotted Eagle could not climb up the cliff or lower himself to the ground. He was trapped.

When the old eagles returned, they dove at Spotted Eagle and screeched whenever he moved.

Four days passed. Without food or water, Spotted Eagle became dizzy with hunger and thirst. He tied himself to a boulder so that he would not fall. Then Spotted Eagle looked up into the sky and prayed to the Great Spirit, "*Wakan Tanka*, have pity on me!"

Spotted Eagle fell asleep. He dreamed he was grabbing the young eagles. There was a flash of lightning, and cracks of thunder shook the earth. A black cloud spread across the sky and turned into a great eagle that beat the air with its wings and screeched in the howling wind.

Spotted Eagle heard a high-pitched voice: "You who pray, you will be our brother. You must never harm us. You will have our power, when you need it. But you must use it for your people!"

In the morning, one of the old eagles dropped a rabbit at Spotted Eagle's feet. The two chicks squawked until he shared his meal.

After two moons
—and the sharing of many
rabbits and mice and prairie dogs—the
eagles had grown big enough to fly. They would soon
abandon the nest. If Spotted Eagle were to live, he knew he
would have to fly also.

"Brothers, you have shared your home and your food with me. You are
ready to leave the nest, and so am I." Spotted Eagle untied his rope and
grabbed the eagles' legs. "We will live together or die together.
Hoka-hey!" And Spotted Eagle jumped.

The two young eagles flapped their wings
wildly as they were pulled
down and down . . .

. . . until Spotted Eagle landed safely on the ground. An eagle feather drifted out of the sky. Spotted Eagle caught it and cried out, "Great Spirit, I am grateful! Winged brothers, I will not forget! One day I will come back with gifts for you!"

Everyone in the village was amazed to see Spotted Eagle alive, but no one was more amazed than Black Crow. He had married Red Bird in the Moon When the Cherries Are Ripe. "How did you escape?" asked Black Crow.

"I flew away," said Spotted Eagle, looking in his brother's eyes. "You left me to die, but I will not fight you now. If there's war with the Pawnee, every warrior will be needed."

Spotted Eagle spoke truly. Early one morning, the village was attacked by a huge Pawnee war party. Spotted Eagle and Black Crow flew into battle with the speed of an eagle and the cunning of a crow. The outnumbered Lakota fought fiercely to give their women, children, and old ones time to escape. Soon, only Black Crow and Spotted Eagle remained.

A flurry of arrows hit Black Crow's horse. Black Crow tumbled to the ground, crying out to Spotted Eagle, "Brother, forgive me for what I did! Take me on your horse before I am killed!"

"No," answered Spotted Eagle. "Long ago you swore to defend your people, to fight to the end. Meet the enemy where you stand! Then, I will forgive you whether you live or die."

"I will earn your forgiveness," said Black Crow. "I will fight where I stand. *Hoka-hey!* It is a good day to die!"

Black Crow died a warrior's death, and so did many of the
Pawnee. At last, the enemy rode off with the herd of captured
Lakota horses.

"Your husband died well," Spotted Eagle told Red Bird.
And the Lakota mourned the death of their warriors through
the long winter.

One morning in the Moon of the Grass Appearing, Spotted Eagle braided an eagle feather into his hair and rode back to the bluff where he had flown with the eagles.

The nest was gone. He lit his sacred pipe, pointing it to the West and the North, the East and the South, up to the Great Spirit and down to Grandmother Earth . . .

"*Wakan Tanka*, accept my offerings! Eagle brothers, hear me! I have come to thank you!" Spiraling down from the clouds came two eagles, gliding closer and closer . . .

. . . and landing at his feet. Spotted Eagle gave them gifts of buffalo meat. He tied tiny medicine bundles on their legs as a sign of friendship between the Eagle nation and the Lakota nation. Then Spotted Eagle watched the eagles soar away on the wind and disappear.

Spotted Eagle and Red Bird were married in the Moon of the Falling Leaves.

Both Spotted Eagle and Black Crow
were brave warriors, but only one
went the way of *wakan*,
only one remembered the wisdom
of things of the spirit . . .
and in the end only one
lived to give thanks
to *Wakan Tanka*, the Great Spirit,
and to the *Wanblee*,
our winged brothers.